Will I Have a Friend?

By Miriam Cohen
Illustrated by Ronald Himler

Published in the United States of America by Star Bright Books, Inc.,
30-19 48th Avenue, Long Island City, NY 11101.

The name Star Bright Books and the Star Bright Books logo are registered
trademarks of Star Bright Books, Inc. Please visit www.starbrightbooks.com.
For bulk orders, please email orders@starbrightbooks.com

ISBN-13: 978-1-59572-069-6

Previously published under ISBN 0027227901

Printed in China (WKT) 9 8 7 6 5 4 3 2 1

Library of Congress Cataloging-in-Publication Data

Cohen, Miriam, 1926-
Will I have a friend? / by Miriam Cohen ; illustrated by Ronald Himler.
p. cm.
Summary: Jim's anxieties on his first day of school are happily forgotten when he
makes a new friend.
ISBN 978-1-59572-069-6 (hardcover : alk. paper)
[1. Frist day of school--Fiction. 2. Schools--Fiction. 3. Friendship--Fiction.]
I. Himler, Ronald, ill. II. Title.
PZ7.C6628Wi 2009

[E]--dc22
2008036957

To Monroe, Adam, Gabriel, and Jem

When Pa was taking Jim to school for the first time,
Jim said, "Will I have a friend at school?"
"I think you will," said Dad.
And Pa smiled down at him.

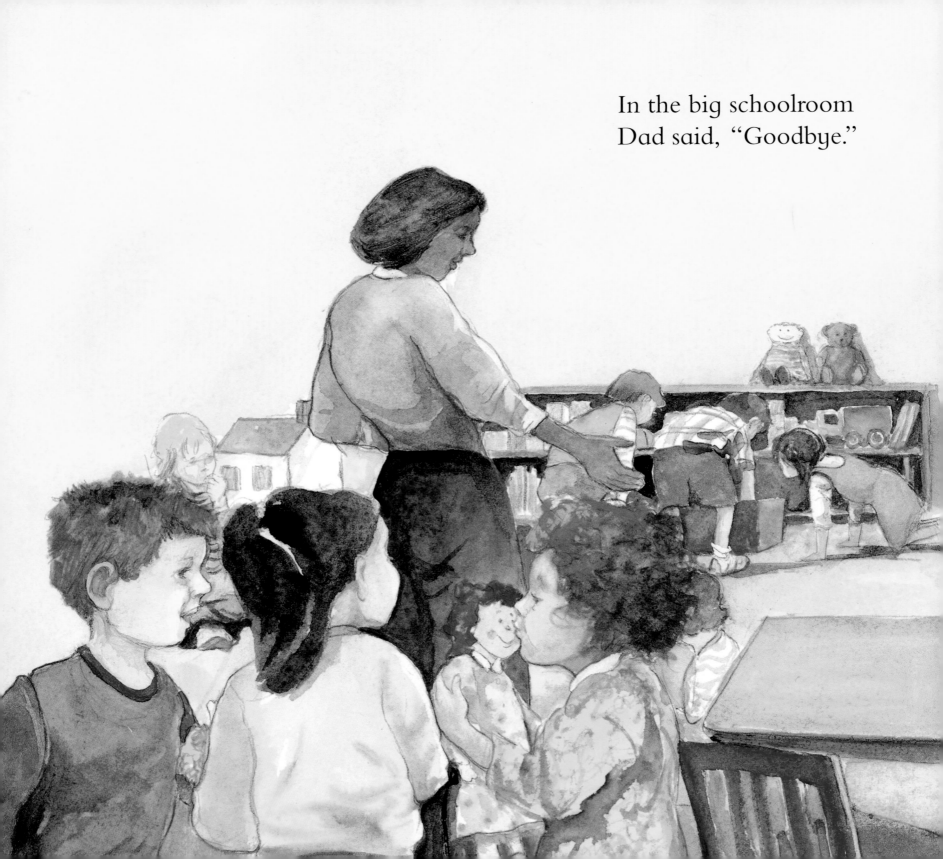

In the big schoolroom
Dad said, "Goodbye."

Jim didn't say anything.
He didn't want to say good-bye.
"Come, Jim," the teacher said.

All the boys were making noise.
All the girls were laughing.
Where was his friend?

The teacher said, "Here is Bill.
He is a rocket man." Bill said, "Rrrrr,"
and he rocketed off.

Anna-Maria walked by.
She was pulling a wagon filled with blocks.
Jim looked at them.
Anna-Maria skipped away.

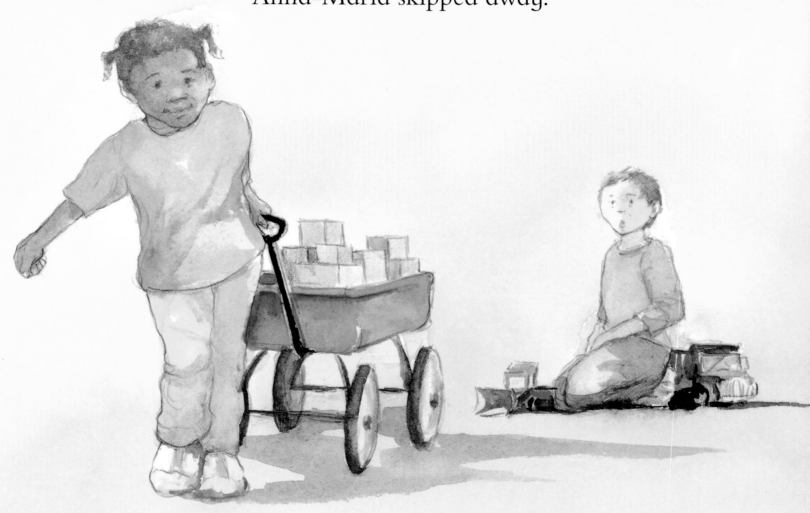

Jim went over to the big table.
There were lumps and humps of colorful clay on it.
The children were pulling and pinching,
poking and patting the clay.

They were making snakes, hills, holes and a banana.
Jim reached out and touched the clay.
It was cool and wet. When he picked it up, it was heavy.

Jim made a man.
But he did not have a friend to show him to.

Now it was orange juice and cookie time.
George said, "I want to pass the cookies!"
"Look!" shouted Bill. "I bit the moon!"
"So did I," said Anna-Maria.

Jim thought of something to say. He said it to Joseph.
But Joseph's mouth was full of cookies. He didn't answer.
The pitcher was empty. Juice time was over.

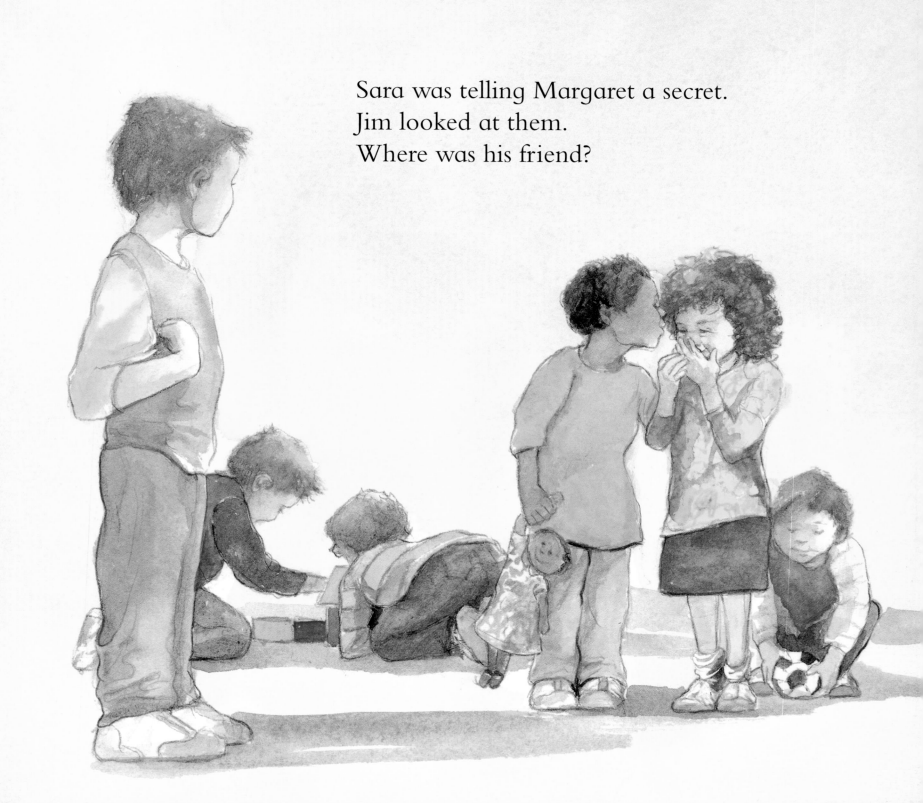

Sara was telling Margaret a secret.
Jim looked at them.
Where was his friend?

Danny was shouting, "Let's do funny tummies!"
Danny poked out his tummy and bumped Willy's.
Willy bumped Sammy's.

When they bumped they laughed and
yelled, "Hello, Mr. Funny Tummy!"
And Jim laughed, too.

The teacher called, "Come to story time!"
All the children came running. Jim sat next to Paul.
The teacher read them a book about a monkey.

Danny jumped up. "I'm a monkey!" he said.
He put his tongue in his lip, and stuck his fingers in his ears.
Jim thought he looked just like a monkey.

The teacher said, "It's time for monkeys to rest."
They lay down on their mats.
It was hard for them to lie still.

Jim looked at the ceiling. He scratched his foot.
Then he rolled over. Then he rolled back.
Someone was looking at him. It was Paul.
He had something in his hand.

When rest time was over, everyone got up.
"Look what I have," said Paul.
He showed Jim a tiny truck.

Jim reached out and Paul put it in his hand.
"The doors really work," said Paul.
"I have a gas pump," said Jim.
"I'll bring it tomorrow."

Anna-Maria called, "Jim and Paul!
Don't you want to play?"
"OK, Jim?" asked Paul.
"OK!" said Jim.

"I thought you would," said Dad.
And Dad smiled down at him.

After school, skipping home,
Jim said to Dad, "Do you know what?
I have a friend at school."